NEVADA PUBLIC LIBRARY

P9-ELT-479

ER O'CONNOR

07/01

O'Connor, Teddy, 1984-
A new brain for Igor.

A NO

When   ding,   ving
them t   hem   ight
food t   ting
stories   vely   rful
illustra   the   iefs   and
worthw   ie. Th   ntire
library   ning
readers   ith a sh

Ear   Step   for
brand-   two
lines o   ook to   the
same   ing
Books   are
both l   **oks**
introd   plot
lines.

Nevada Public Library
631 K Avenue
Nevada, Iowa 50201
515-382-2628

increa
The   ool
throug   ool
throug   2,
grades   for
Step 4   ove
throug   eps
over a   DEMCO   will
help y

For my mother
—T.O.

To the memory of my Master,
Raymond Ameijide, illustrator,
from his grateful and loyal apprentice
—B.B.

Text copyright © 2001 by Teddy O'Connor. Illustrations copyright © 2001 by Bill Basso.
All rights reserved under International and Pan-American Copyright Conventions.
Published in the United States by Random House, Inc., New York, and simultaneously in
Canada by Random House of Canada Limited, Toronto.
www.randomhouse.com/kids
Library of Congress Cataloging-in-Publication Data
O'Connor, Teddy, 1984–
A new brain for Igor / by Teddy O'Connor ; illustrated by Bill Basso.
  p. cm. — (Step into reading. A step 1 book)
SUMMARY: A mad scientist's dim-witted assistant tries to force his master into giving him a bigger
brain by stealing the scientist's fuzzy pink slippers.
ISBN 0-375-80626-1 (trade) — ISBN 0-375-90626-6 (lib. bdg.)
[1. Scientists—Fiction.] I. Basso, Bill, ill. II. Title. III. Step into reading. Step 1 book.
PZ7.O2227 Ng 2001 [E]—dc21 00-038711
Printed in the United States of America July 2001 10 9 8 7 6 5 4 3 2 1
STEP INTO READING, Random House, and the Random House colophon are registered trademarks
and the Step into Reading colophon is a trademark of Random House, Inc.

Step into Reading®

A New Brain for Igor

By Teddy O'Connor

Illustrated by Bill Basso

A Step 1 Book

Random House 🏠 New York

Nevada Public Library

BEEP!

BEEP!

This is Igor.

He works for Master.

Igor wants to be smart
like Master.

But Igor's brain is
very small.

Master can make robots.

Igor can't even make paper dolls.

Master can wake
the dead.

Igor can't even wake
his hamster, Peggy.

Igor is unhappy.
"I want to be smart
like Master,"
he tells Peggy.
"I want a new brain.
A big brain.
But how can I
make Master
give me one?"

SMART MAN BRAIN

PICKLE

Igor thinks and thinks.
Then he smiles
a sly smile.
Igor has a plan!

DOG BRAIN

CAT BRAIN

DINOSAUR BRAIN

Igor follows Master
all around the lab.
What does Master
love best?
More than anything,
Master loves his
fuzzy pink slippers.
His grammy gave them
to him.

That night
Igor creeps
into Master's room.

Master is asleep.
Igor takes off
the fuzzy pink slippers.

Master wakes up.
"What are you doing
with my
fuzzy pink slippers?
Give them back!"

Igor runs
out of the room.
He hides Master's
fuzzy pink slippers.

"Give me a big new brain. Then I will give back your fuzzy pink slippers!" Igor shouts.

Master looks everywhere
for his fuzzy
pink slippers.

He looks under
Igor's bed.

He looks in Igor's closet.

No slippers!

He looks
in the
fridge.

He looks
in the
shower.

He even checks the toilet!
The slippers are nowhere
to be found!

Master sobs
and sobs.

"My grammy gave me those slippers. I must have them! I will give you a new brain!" Master cries.

Master puts Igor
on a table.
Igor is asleep.

He takes out Igor's small brain.

He puts in a new,
bigger brain.

A little later
Igor wakes up.

He jumps up and down.

He is so happy.

Yes!

He has a new brain...

a bigger brain...

…a doggy brain!
He licks Master's face.
He pants with joy.
"Good boy, Igor,"
says Master.
"Now fetch my
fuzzy pink slippers."

And Igor does.